DESTINY

DESTINY

The Little Helper

Jana Anderson and Darryl Anderson

Illustrated by Darryl Anderson

DEA & J Publishing
Lansing, Michigan

DEA & J Publishing
Lansing, Michigan
DEAandJPublishing@gmail.com

Printed and bound in the United States of America
ISBN: 978-1-7353985-0-1 (Paperback Edition)
ISBN: 978-1-7353985-1-8 (Hardcover Edition)
ISBN: 978-1-7353985-3-2 (E-book Edition)

IN LOVING MEMORY
of our fathers Carstell Peeples and Lawrence Anderson

AND TO OUR FAMILY
for all of your love and support, including our nieces and nephews who have helped us see the world from a child's point-of-view

Hi! My name is Destiny and I'm six years old.

I live with my mama, daddy, sister, brother, and our grandmother—Nana Daisy.

I'm very smart and I love helping my family with chores around our home.

Sometimes the grass in our yard grows really tall and Daddy cuts it with the orange lawn mower.

Before he mows the lawn, I pick up all of the big rocks and sticks so that they don't get run over.

Daddy gives me a thumbs up and tells me I did a great job.

Now, he can cut the grass.

While Daddy finishes the lawn, I go back inside and get cleaned up.

Mama is cooking dinner, so I help her by putting the empty food boxes and vegetable scraps in the trash can.

We're having beef stew tonight—my favorite!

Baby Brother, Micah, wants to help, too. But he's not big enough yet.

"It's okay, Baby Brother. You can help when you're older."

I hand him his bottle, but he just cries and screams and throws it on the floor.

I try to cover my ears because Micah's screams are really loud and they are making my head hurt.

Now is a good time to go and see what Nana Daisy is doing.

I find Nana Daisy in the dining room setting the table for dinner.

"Destiny, will you please grab some silverware?" she asks.

"Oh, and three more bowls . . . and one more cup."

"Yes, Nana. I'll go get them now."

"Thank you, Baby!"

Dinner was delicious! Now, it's time to cleanup.

Nana stacks a pile of dirty plates and cups in my arms.
Then, I walk slowly to the kitchen to make sure that I don't
drop them.

"Thank you, Little Sis!" says my big sister Deja as I hand
her the pile.

My favorite chore is cleaning off the dining room table.

The table makes a funny noise when I wipe it with the wet cloth.

Squeak, squeak, squeak, squeak!

Nana Daisy says that I'm the best table cleaner ever!

After I wipe off the table, Daddy vacuums the floor.

He is pretty good at vacuuming, but I want to make sure that he doesn't miss anything.

I get on my hands and knees. Then, I point out things on the floor that need to be vacuumed.

"Look! Over here, Daddy!"

Baby Brother, Micah, had a lot of fun playing in his room.

Daddy is about to give him a bath, so I help Micah put his toys away.

But Baby Brother is not ready for the fun to end. He wants to play some more.

"Nooooo! Want play!" Micah yells.

While Micah is taking a bath, I go downstairs to the basement to help Mama, Nana, and Deja fold laundry.

Deja throws a sheet over my head that's too big for me to fold by myself, so I run around and pretend I'm a ghost.

I don't remember what sound a ghost makes, so I start barking like a dog.

"Woof! Woof! Woof! Woof!" I bark, as I waive my arms in the air.

Deja is cracking up laughing.

It's been a long day, but now that the chores are done, it's time to sit back and relax.

I kiss Nana Daisy good night before she goes to bed.

Then, I go to the living room to hang out with the rest of the family for a while.

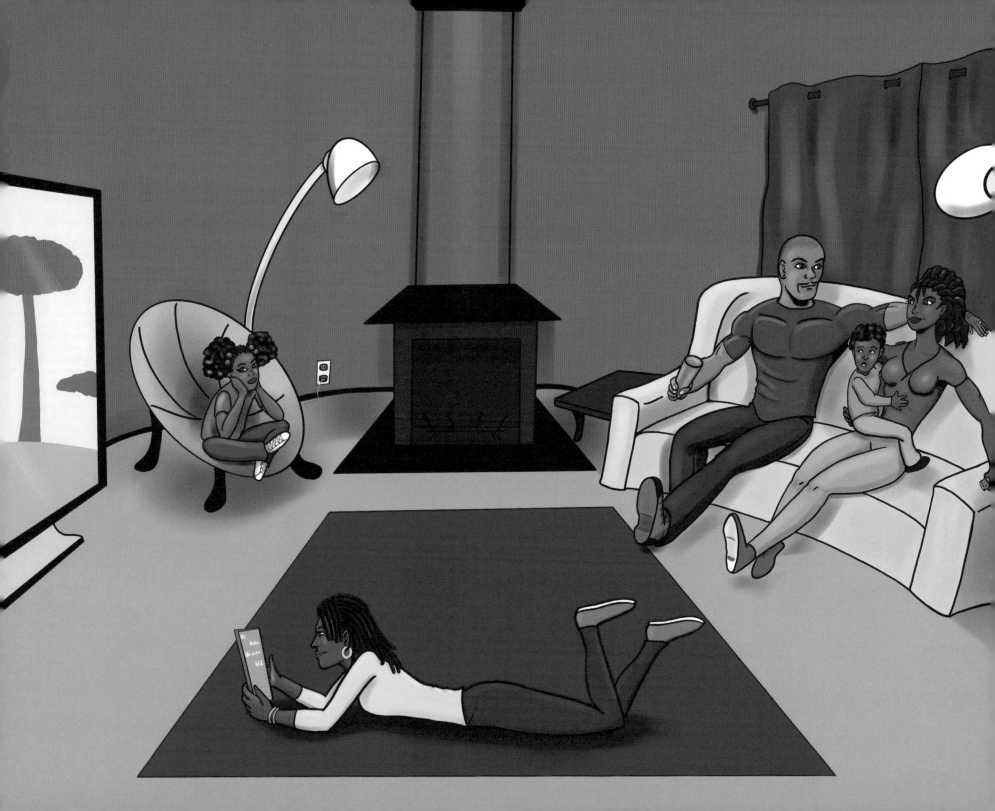

When it's time for bed, I go to my room and Mama and Daddy come to tuck me in.

After we say our prayers, Daddy reads me a story. As he is reading, my eyes get really sleepy and I can hardly stay awake.

"Good night, Baby Girl. Thank you for always being so helpful around the house," Mama says as they stand up to leave.

"Yes. Thank you, Destiny," Daddy agrees as he kisses my forehead. "We love you very much."

"Good night. I love you, too," I tell them, yawning. "I can't wait to see what new things I can help with tomorrow!"

CPSIA information can be obtained at www.ICGtesting.com
Printed in the USA
LVIW012153061020
668147LV00002B/8